MW01166764

LIVING WELL

SLEEPING
FOR GOOD HEALTH

by Shirley Wimbish Gray

THE CHILD'S WORLD®
CHANHASSEN, MINNESOTA

The Child's World®

Published in the United States of America by The Child's World®
P.O. Box 326, Chanhassen, MN 55317-0326
800-599-READ
www.childsworld.com

Subject Consultant:
Diana Ruschhaupt,
Director of Programs,
Ruth Lilly Health
Education Center,
Indianapolis,
Indianapolis

Photo Credits: Cover: Brand X Pictures/Creatas; Corbis: 5 (Paul A. Sounders), 9, 10 (LWA-Dann Tardif), 11 (Trinette Reed), 11 right (Barbara Peacock), 12 (Ariel Skelley), 13 (Françoise Gervais), 15, 16 (Tom Stewart), 19 (Lester V. Bergman), 20 (Rob Lewine), 21 (Owen Franken), 23 (Tom & Dee Ann McCarthy), 24, 25 right (Jose Luis Pelaez Inc.), 27 (Ronnie Kaufman), 29 (Steve Kaufman); Custom Medical Stock Pictures: 17, 18, 22; PhotoEdit: 6 (Michael Newman), 14 (Jeff Greenberg), 25 (Bill Aron), 26 (Eric Fowke); Punchstock: 7 (Digital Vision), 8 (Hollingsworth).

The Child's World®: Mary Berendes, Publishing Director

Editorial Directions, Inc.: E. Russell Primm, Editorial Director; Elizabeth K. Martin, Line Editor; Katie Marsico, Assistant Editor; Olivia Nellums, Editorial Assistant; Susan Hindman, Copy Editor; Sarah E. De Capua, Proofreader; Peter Garnham and Chris Simms, Fact Checkers; Tim Griffin/IndexServ, Indexer; Elizabeth K. Martin and Matthew Messbarger, Photo Researchers and Selectors

Library of Congress Cataloging-in-Publication Data
Gray, Shirley W.
Sleeping for good health / by Shirley Wimbish Gray.
     p. cm.—(Living well)
Includes index.
Contents: A good night's sleep!—What happens when you sleep?—
How much sleep do you need?—Learning about sleep—When sleep
is a problem—Get your rest!
  ISBN 1-59296-080-4 (lib. bdg. : alk. paper)
 1. Sleep—Juvenile literature. 2. Children—Sleep—Juvenile literature.
[1. Sleep.] I. Title. II. Series: Living well (Child's World (Firm))
  RA786.G73 2004
  612.8'21—dc21
                                        2003006278

TABLE OF CONTENTS

CHAPTER ONE

A GOOD NIGHT'S SLEEP!

Kristen feels tired as she takes off her ballet shoes at the end of class. "Be sure to get plenty of sleep tonight," her teacher tells the class. "I want everyone to do their best at the recital tomorrow."

Kristen wants to have a friend over to spend the night, but she decides against it. Instead, she has dinner with her family and reads a book. Then she goes to bed and falls asleep quickly. In the morning, she feels great. She is ready for her dance recital.

Even though Kristen had worked her body hard at practice, she was not tired the next day. Her body rested while she slept. Think of everything you do during the day. Your body needs rest, too.

Kristen was ready for her dance recital after a good night's rest.

CHAPTER TWO

WHAT HAPPENS
WHEN YOU SLEEP?

Sleep is when the body rests. Most of the body's activities slow

down during sleep. The heart beats slower, and the **blood**

pressure drops. Breathing is deeper and slower. The body is

*Sleep is an essential part of our lives. Good, restful sleep
is needed in order for us to be at our best every single day.*

less likely to respond to noise or other sensations like touch. Even the body's temperature drops during sleep.

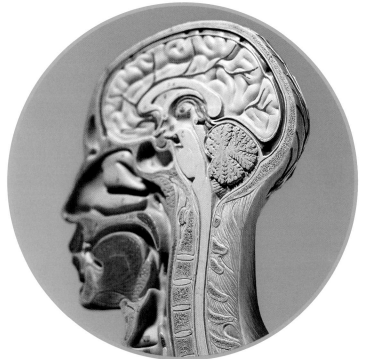

Our brains control our sleep.

Scientists think that sleep is the time when the body repairs itself. The human brain is the control center for sleep. It sends messages to the body as it goes through several stages of sleep each night.

During stage 1, the eyes close and the muscles begin to relax. You may have seen a friend fall into this first stage of sleep at school. As your friend's muscles relax, her head may drop or her pencil may fall from her hand. If you gently touch your friend, she

should wake up easily before the teacher notices!

Once the muscles relax, the body moves quickly into stage 2.

This is light sleep, and most people still hear sounds or feel touch at

this point. Next comes a period of deeper sleep. During stage 3, the body does not respond easily to noise or touch. It is also not aware if the air temperature is hot or cold. It is harder to wake someone from this stage than from one of the earlier stages.

Have you ever fallen asleep outside for a little while when the weather is warm and sunny? This is usually referred to as light sleep.

Waking up and getting out of bed is one of the hardest parts of the day for many people.

The deepest sleep occurs in stage 4. Someone who wakes up from this stage will feel groggy and may be confused. Usually a person moves back and forth through all of these stages several times during the night.

What about Animals?

You probably have seen your dog or cat sleep. Do all animals sleep like humans do? The answer is both yes and no. Scientists think that, yes, all animals sleep, but not quite like humans do.

A giraffe, for example, sleeps less than two hours a day. It also sleeps standing up. A brown bat will spend four hours a day hunting for insects. It spends the other 20 hours asleep, hanging by its feet!

The black sea dolphin may be the most unusual. Only half of its brain goes to sleep at a time. The other half is wide-awake. Scientists think this helps the dolphin protect itself by always being alert!

Another stage of sleep is called REM sleep. That stands for Rapid Eye Movement. The muscles are still relaxed, but the body is more active during this stage. The heart may beat faster, and the eyes move back and forth quickly under the eyelids. This is also the stage when dreams occur.

CHAPTER THREE

HOW MUCH
SLEEP DO YOU NEED?

"We will have a big test tomorrow," your teacher says as you

leave school. "Be sure to get enough sleep tonight."

How much sleep is enough? This

depends on how old you are. The

younger you are, the more sleep

your body needs. So a child in

Young children need more sleep than older kids and grown ups (top).
Adults need about eight hours of sleep every night (bottom).

Trying to cram for a test never works. The best way to do well in school is to study and do your homework in advance, not late at night.

kindergarten will need more sleep than a teenager does. A 9- or

10-year-old generally needs about nine hours of sleep. Most adults

need eight hours, but some people need much less.

Getting enough sleeps helps you do your best in school. You

will be able to pay attention to your teacher. You will probably

find that math and reading are easier. You will also be in a better

mood than if you were tired from not getting the right amount

of sleep.

Have you ever had trouble falling asleep? Maybe it was the night before your birthday party, or the day your team won its soccer game. Sometimes it is hard to relax and fall asleep if you are excited when you go to bed. This happens to everyone once in a while.

Have you ever been to a sleepover? Sometimes, trying to go to sleep when you are with your friends is hard because you just want to laugh and play. This makes getting to sleep difficult.

Some people have trouble sleeping almost every night. They have insomnia (in-SOM-nee-uh). That is a Latin word meaning, "not sleep."

Insomnia can be very hard on your body and your mental health.

Insomnia may disappear by itself after several days or weeks. Then the person finds it easy to get enough sleep again. If not, a doctor may be able to find a physical problem that is causing the person not to sleep.

CHAPTER FOUR

HOW DO WE LEARN ABOUT SLEEP?

Doctors have been studying how and why people sleep since the 1800s. At first, some doctors thought that sleep was caused by a lack of blood flowing to the brain. Others thought that poisons built up in the blood during the day. They thought that these poisons caused a person to sleep. When the body got rid of the poisons, the person would wake up.

Today, scientists know that the brain, not the

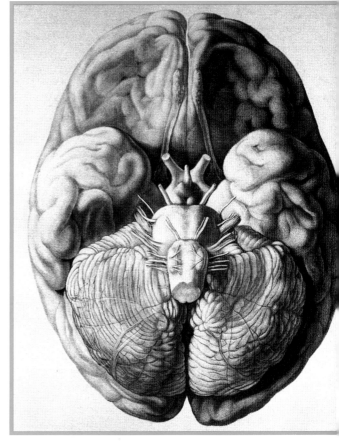

An early scientific drawing of a human brain

blood, controls sleep. They also know that several different chemicals

in the brain are involved. However, they still have many questions.

Why do some people need more sleep than others? How does the body

know when to wake up?

Scientists study sleep in sleep laboratories. These include

soundproof bedrooms where people can sleep all night. The

*Some people need alarm clocks to wake up in the morning,
others simply wake up when they have to.*

Scientists monitor people sleeping to study brain function during sleep.

scientists measure people's brain waves while they are sleeping. In the

morning, the doctors print a graph. It shows the different stages of

sleep each person went through during the night. The lines on the

graph will go up and down like a roller coaster. Looking at these

graphs has helped scientists learn about sleep. They now know that the

brain does not slow down during sleep. It stays active. This activity

helps us think clearly and solve problems while we are awake.

CHAPTER FIVE

WHEN IS
SLEEP A PROBLEM?

Doctors in the field of sleep medicine help people who have

trouble going to sleep or staying asleep. For example, some children

and adults have trouble getting a good night's sleep because of

breathing problems. They may have sleep apnea (AP-nee-ya).

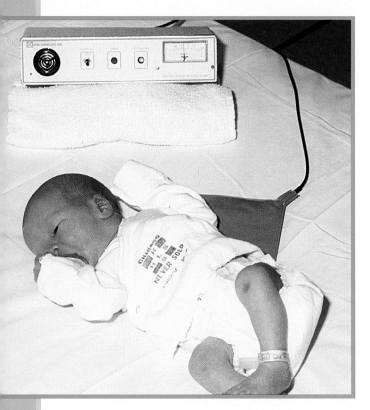

Apnea is a Greek word

that means "without wind."

A child who has apnea will

stop breathing for 20 sec-

onds or more. Then breath-

ing starts again. This may

happen several times dur-

ing the night.

Baby with apnea monitor (above)

Snoring is a common sign that someone has apnea. Sometimes large **tonsils** or **adenoids** block the windpipe and cause the problem. If these are removed, then the child should sleep easily again. In adults, losing weight may help the apnea disappear.

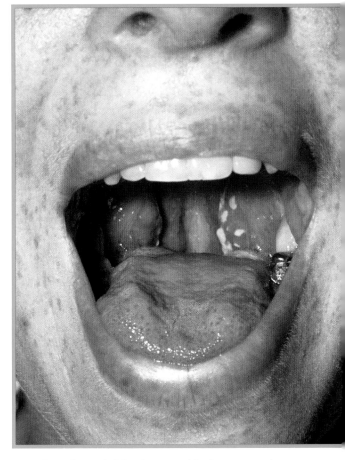

Enlarged tonsils like these can block your windpipe and keep you from sleeping well.

Sometimes, children and adults have nightmares while they are asleep. Nightmares are dreams that are scary. They occur during REM sleep. Usually a child who wakes up from a nightmare can remember exactly what happened in the dream.

Night terrors are different from nightmares. Night terrors happen in young children between the ages of three and five. The child may wake up screaming or crying in fear. Even though his eyes are open, the child is still asleep. The terror may last a few minutes or even an hour. In the morning, the child will not remember being scared.

Another common sleep problem for children is sleepwalking. This usually happens during stage 3 or 4 sleep early in the night.

When you were younger, you probably experienced night terrors.

Narcoleptics can fall asleep just about anywhere at anytime.

A sleepwalker is asleep but looks or acts awake. Sleepwalkers can get

dressed, walk around the house, or even go outside without waking

up. In the morning, the child will not remember sleepwalking.

Usually, children outgrow night terrors and sleepwalking.

Sometimes people have trouble staying awake. They may have

narcolepsy (NAR-ko-lep-see). People with this problem cannot keep

Dream the Night Away

Why do we dream? Scientists are not sure. Some think that this is the brain's way of storing information it gathered during the day. Others think this is when the brain solves problems from the day.

Everybody dreams at night, but not everybody remembers their dreams in the morning. If you wake up during REM sleep, you will probably remember many details about your dreams. If you wake up during another stage of sleep, you will not. Some people say they dream in color. Others say they only dream in black and white. What did you dream last night?

from suddenly falling asleep. This happens no matter where they are or what they are doing. They may fall asleep at the dinner table or while driving a car. They may fall asleep for a few minutes or for a few hours. A doctor can help a person with narcolepsy control the condition.

CHAPTER SIX

How Can You Sleep Better?

After a full day of playing and working, most children fall asleep as soon as their heads hit their pillows. There are several things you can do to make sure that sleep comes easily for you.

Do you fall fast asleep as soon as you go to bed?
If you do, it's a sign that you've had a full, active day.

Watch what you eat and when you eat. Drinks with **caffeine** can keep you awake. The best thing is not to drink colas, hot chocolate, or tea after dinner.

Most soft drinks have caffeine in them. If you want to get a good night's rest, it's best not to drink soda after dinner.

Healthy snacks such as crackers, fruit, nuts, and cheese are good to eat if you are hungry and it's near your bedtime (top). Instead of soda, try having a glass of warm milk before bedtime (right).

Sometimes, eating a big meal before bedtime keeps you awake. If you are hungry, try a small snack such as crackers and cheese. Some people say a glass of warm milk helps them go to sleep.

What you do before bedtime also makes a difference.

Reading a book is a good way to relax. So is taking a warm bath.

Watching a scary movie or TV show will make it harder to relax

and fall asleep.

Getting plenty of exercise during the day is a great way to

make sure you will sleep well at night. Playing sports or a game of

Reading is a great way to unwind. If you need to relax before bedtime, try reading a book.

Don't play too close to your bedtime. You want to be able to go to bed relaxed so that you can get a good night's rest.

hide-and-seek after dinner may be fun, but these activities can also get your heart pumping hard right before bedtime. Give your body time to cool down and slow down before you go to bed. In the morning, you should be able to wake up easily and be ready to go!

Glossary

adenoids (AD-uh-noyds) Adenoids are tissues that are located above the throat, at the back of the nose. They trap germs and prevent them from entering the body.

blood pressure (BLUHD PRESH-ur) Blood pressure is the measure of how hard the heart is pumping and moving blood through the body.

caffeine (KAF-een) Caffeine is a chemical found in coffee, tea, colas, and chocolate that stimulates the brain. Many adults drink coffee in the morning to help them wake up.

sensations (sen-SAY-shuhns) Sensations are feelings, like the touch of a hand.

soundproof (SOUND-proof) Soundproof describes a room that does not allow any sound in or out of it.

tonsils (TON-suhlz) Tonsils are two lumps of tissue located on each side of the back of the throat. They help prevent germs from entering the body.

Questions and Answers about Sleep

How long do babies sleep? A human baby will sleep about 16 hours a day.

How much sleep does a school-age child need? A school-age child needs about nine hours of sleep a day.

How much sleep does an adult need? An adult needs between seven and eight hours of sleep a day.

Can you sleep with your eyes open? Yes, some people can.

What should I do if one night I'm not able to get enough sleep?
Many people believe a nap as short as 15 minutes can help you feel better, but it doesn't replace a full night's sleep.

Did You Know?

▶ Hibernation is a form of deep sleeping that helps certain warm-blooded mammals live through the winter. Bears, woodchucks, and bats are animals that hibernate.

▶ Restless Leg Syndrome (RLS) is a sleep problem that keeps some people from falling asleep at night. They have a tingling feeling in their legs and feel like they need to get up and walk around.

▶ Some animals are nocturnal, which means they are active at night and sleep during the day. Raccoons, opossums, and bats are nocturnal animals.

▶ Humans spend one-third of their lives asleep.

▶ Going to bed at the same time each night helps the body fall asleep more quickly.

This North American brown bear and her cub are sleeping.
Bears are one kind of animal that hibernates during the winter months.

How to Learn More about Sleep

At the Library: Nonfiction
Facklam, Margery, and Pamela Johnson (illustrator). *Do Not Disturb: The Mysteries of Animal Hibernation and Sleep.* San Francisco: Sierra Club Books, 1989.

Fowler, Allan. *A Good Night's Sleep.*
Danbury, Conn.: Children's Press, 1996.

McGinty, Alice B. *Staying Healthy: Sleep and Rest.*
New York: PowerKids Press, 1997.

Riha, Susanne. *Animals at Rest: Sleeping Patterns and Habits.*
Woodbridge, Conn.: Blackbirch Press, 1999.

Silverstein, Alvin, Virginia Silverstein, and Laura Silverstein Nunn. *Sleep.*
Danbury, Conn.: Franklin Watts, 2000.

At the Library: Fiction
Levine, Gail Carson, and Mark Elliot (illustrator). *Princess Sonora and the Long Sleep.*
New York: HarperCollins, 1999.

Prelutsky, Jack, and Yossi Abolafia (illustrator). *My Parents Think I'm Sleeping.*
New York: Greenwillow Books, 1985.

Wong, Janet S., and Julie Paschkis. *Night Garden: Poems from the World of Dreams.*
New York: M. K. McElderry Books, 2000.

On the Web
Visit our home page for lots of links about sleep:
http://www.childsworld.com/links.html

Note to Parents, Teachers, and Librarians: We routinely verify our Web links to make sure they're safe, active sites—so encourage your readers to check them out!

Through the Mail or by Phone

American Sleep Apnea Association
1424 K Street, N.W.
Suite 302
Washington, DC 20005
202/293-3650

Narcolepsy Network, Inc.
10921 Reed Hartman Highway
Cincinnati, OH 45242
513/ 891-3522

National Center on Sleep Disorders Research
P.O. Box 30105
Bethesda, MD 20824-0105
301/592-8573

National Sleep Foundation
1522 K Street, N.W.
Suite 500
Washington, DC 20005
202/347-3471

Restless Leg Syndrome (RLS) Foundation, Inc.
819 Second Street, N.W.
Rochester, MN 55902

Index

About the Author

Shirley Wimbish Gray has been a writer and educator for more than 25 years and has published more than a dozen nonfiction books for children. She also coordinates cancer education programs at the University of Arkansas for Medical Sciences and consults as a writer with scientists and physicians. She lives with her husband and two sons in Little Rock, Arkansas.